The Effect of Moonlight on Tombstones

The Dark Poetry of

Della Van Hise

Eye Scry Publications - 2015
www.eyescry.com

For the muses who sing
the gnosis of vampyres...

And most of all, for Wendy.

Moments Frozen In Time
(A Foreword by the Author)

Poetry has never been something I consciously set out to write. Instead, it is something that comes or not, entirely at the whim of whatever it is that writers call "the muse." Over the years, I have come to think of my own poetry as a form of shorthand - an attempt to capture a moment frozen in time. A wayward leaf caught in mid-fall. A glimpse of a shadow cast by nothing at all. The effect of moonlight on tombstones.

Though I write primarily novels and nonfiction, I do find myself pleasantly haunted by what my mentor once referred to as "the gnosis of vampyres." What does that mean? In essence, I would say it is the voice of silent knowing - the observer within all of us who possesses the ability to see the world clearly, and at times perhaps *too* clearly. As another dear friend once said, "Poetry is the streaming download from the broken heart of the universe." I have found that to be true, at least in my own humble attempts at the art form.

The poems in this anthology represent approximately two decades of those streaming downloads, most of which were scribbled hastily and in bad penmanship into cloth journals. If I have been at all successful in capturing some of those moments frozen in time, perhaps a line or two will resonate with you, hopefully bringing a smile to your face or a chill to your spine.

At the very least, enjoy the dark side of the light.

Della Van Hise
November 8, 2015

TABLE OF CONTENTS

The Effect of Moonlight on Tombstones

Illumination

The shadows have gone walking tonight,
searching for men who once wore them.
On gravestones they linger,
counting blades of amber grass,
gathering the scent of wilted flowers.
A streetlight blossoms
over asphalt gardens,
petals of orange falling through fog
to illumine the lostlings
dancing the edge of the road.

Double Life

I kiss my evil twin,
pressing warm mortal lips
to cold silver ones
above the sink.
Her tongue is a sliver,
a broken mirror cutting deep
to feed her cardinal thirst.
When my eyes open
she's already gone,
the looking glass empty.
I lick the red pane clean,
trying to find myself again.

Burnt Offering

Melted wax,
red blood of candlelight
shed at the vampyre altar,
liquid silk searing satin nipple,
pain an ascending descent
into heavenly hell—
my beacon, my thirteen leather lashes,
my cry into the crack
between sunset and forever.
A burning wick whispers,
      "This is the dark evolution."
Day sizzles, dissolves.
I ride the candles into the night,
the sacrifice seeking the blade.

Transformation

Coyote sings the night alive,
mad dog hymns of immortality
etched on obsidian metal sky.
I question what I am:
        passive audience to the song?
        a minor note in the chorus?
        Nothing at all?
The singing ends,
the world goes still.
My hands are disappearing.

The Dark Red Mass

This is his immortal body:
  leather wings
  October leaves
  stones of fallen bridges
  a teacup from *Titanic*
  dust from the bones of kings
  archaic ruins
  asteroids and ashes.
Eat of this
and we will outlive time.

This is his blood:
  extract of dark dreams
  tide swells of Styx
  dew from a pumpkin patch
  acid rain in black goblets
  milk from the nipples of witches
  tears of weeping icons
  wet woe of slashed wrists
  dampness of virgins
  sallow seed of sinful priests.
Drink it deep
so we will never die.

Assassin

My soul went running in the hills again
on bare bloody feet.
Death is stalking me,
and I do not forgive God
for creating an assassin
to carry out the contract.
        "Thou shalt not kill."

Falling Stars

The moon climbed a cold sky tonight,
ladder of broken clouds ascending.
Heaven is raining vampyre hearts,
falling stars that crack the night.
My dreams fracture, too,
inviting you in.

Time and Tragedy

There's a mockingbird singing arias to the midnight
while coyotes cry in dead shamans' voices
and a comet plays sinister pinball with Mars.
My window is a theater
where time and tragedy paint themselves
on the black fabric screen
of the night that never ends.
Mortal still,
I read the deepening lines,
messages on my mirror,
and deeper in the dark
I wonder how the play will end.

Fallen Angel

Are the stars really campfires
on the shores of heaven,
lit by lost souls waiting,
or did you forget to put out the lights
when God threw you out of his bed
for night after ever-after-night,
fallen vampyre angel?
No matter, my love,
I've built a finer fire to warm you,
a blaze of candles to lead you home.
Heaven, after all,
is only for the dead.

Vampyreland

I dreamed you into Be-ing
and gave you half my heart.
You took it, bleeding,
to vampyreland
so I would be always drawn there,
moth to flame,
moon to night,
heart to beat.
You are the reflection
who fled from the mirror.

*

The tree of life
sunk its roots
in the cold black earth
at the edge of vampyreland.
The cemeteries are subdivisions,
the headstones only door knockers
to the far side of time.

*

In vampyreland
ravens and bats are sacrosanct citizens
with hidden agendas.
Canaries are shunned,
along with the sun,
and yellow is not permitted
in a child's box of crayons.

*

The vampyre cathedral is built
over the powdered bones
of the King of Halloween.
At night, skeletons dance on
popsicle stick stages,
admiring jagged smiles
in stained glass caskets.

*

The streetlights here
weep glass tears,
blinded by scoundrels
defending the chastity of night.

*

I collect darkling dreams
in little bottles,
magickal antidotes
to dayshine maladies.

*

The churches here
have no altars
and communion is served
from the torn wrist
of a pagan priest.

*

Mysterious messages appear
in my cloth diary,
scripted in blood.
A cut stings my finger
and though the handwriting is mine,
I don't know the language,
don't remember the words.

The Vampyre King

The vampyre king must be defined
by the grams of magick in a raindrop,
by filigree faerie wings in snowflakes,
by the number of thorns in his crown,
by broken clocks and stopped watches
and crumbling tombstones guarding empty crypts
etched with the names of the men he has been.

Black Book

The night is a black book
written in invisible ink,
full of alchemy recipes.
Between the pages
obsidian orchids are pressed,
staining tissue paper sky
with a pollen of stars.
When all the blooms have fallen
like angels from heaven,
I will be no closer to death.

Grim Little Snippets

Webs on my altar
define the nature of time.
Flame rewrites the dream.

The raven's black eye
projects all reality.
If he blinks, we die.

Candles keep journals
of time's passing
in empty books of matches.

I keep the stars in my coffin
   only letting them out at night..
Sometimes, sadly,
   they fall.

I envy your coffin bed,
wanting you to lie down
inside me
instead.

Night is a poem
written in ebony ink
on eternity's torn page.

I do not believe
the hag in the mirror is me.
The glass has surely
withered.

Faith makes us docile
in the face of our own death.
Mortal indulgence.

My sheets are cold and black.
The storm prince smells of ash and apples.
Winter falls.

Paintings On the Devil's Inner Eye

There's an angel hiding by the wood pile
in the guise of an abandoned shirt,
and the bones spell a warning
that winter is coming early November.
Brittle nettles,
tall grass blown brown,
shadows tangling in Celtic knots
to tie the world together.
These are the spirits I summon.
This is the season of fog
and blood on the thorns of roses,
dusk in dragon faerie land,
paintings on the devil's inner eye,
sanctuary and monastery,
far more real
than the realm of mortal man.

Stained Glass Dreaming

Somewhere in this hollowed out pumpkin
I breathed myself into being
and called it Life.
It's all just a grand cotillion
thrown by the gods
to honor our existence.
But midnight comes all too soon
and the prince drinks blood
from a crystal slipper
while the princess eats a poison mushroom
and sleeps forever in a stained glass coffin
dreaming of dreaming of being
alive.

Mortal Machinations

Fat half moon
illumines a half-formed world
where mechanical phantom families
dance happily atop white picket fences
which become grave markers
all too quickly.

Fragile Sanctuary

My heart is a haunted room,
sinister sanctuary.
When it breaks,
shattered by your sharp white smile,
all the shadows come leaking out,
phantoms of neverland
loosed on the world of men.

Harvest

I dine on purple twilight,
suckling gathering dusk,
a feast to sustain the darkness
when the cold sun rises.

My garden grows only thistles.
Daydreams planted in idle youth
lie like corpses in the ground.
Nightmares are my aspirations now,
precious harvest,
sweet as a lover's blood.

Outcasts

The guardian angels of circus freaks
perch on wrought iron cages,
preening red and white canvas wings
with cardboard cones
salvaged from dropped cotton candy.
Deformed, mute and bitter,
they build stairways to Hell
where the damned seek sanctuary
and broken seraphim
plot vengeance against the light.

Paradox xodaraP

Mockingbird songs and echoes
are only silences in the abyss,
faded lithographs.
Here the vampyre finds his reflection,
visible only in darkness
where all enlightenment exists.

Embers

The stars are so much glitter
spilt on the canvas of the abyss,
their light only a reflection
of campfires left dying
on the rocky shores of Hell.

Quanta

1.
Restless spirits created December
to please you
and keep it for you always
in snowstorm waterball paperweights
where quantum realities reside.

2.
Meteors shower the night:
iron sugar, nickel salt.
Am I only Death's dinner,
seasoned inside this mortal shell,
tenderized by stardust?

3.
The cemetery lies empty,
pallid headstones only coloring books
for the idle hands of time.

Vampyre Season

Cold the vampyre wind
blowing my secrets away.
Eternity waits.

On the edge of dreams
I dangle my sharp hook,
waiting for your bite.

Vampyre king plays house
with dolls cut from human cloth,
ragged souls of lace.

Those Who Wait

The candelabra stands dark,
grieving the passing of time
with hardened wax tears
collected in scarlet rivers.
A cobweb on the ceiling undulates,
restless dry ocean.
Though the windows are all shut
in honor of autumn,
the wind is cold and hungry
and sneaks in thru the cracks,
looking for warmth.
Plastic pumpkins and velvet harlequins
watch the circus unfold,
secretly wondering what will become of them
when the mortal who placed them on the shelf
joins the gathering dust.

Route 66

The darkling king writes poems
on tiny pebbles and sagebrush tea leaves,
leaving them in broken mail boxes
among the ruins of Route 66,
where ghosts of dead motorcyclists
and suicided musicians
come to read their fortunes.

Fingerpainting

There's a black crayon melting
to form a pool of night.
Thick as honey,
hot as blood,
it closes over me
like a coffin lid
and I am swimming
in a fingerpainting
still wet on the walls of Hell.

Past Lives

I have buried all my past lives
in appropriate graves:
    the only child in a doll's house
    drawn to its rest by a little red wagon;
    the sci-fi geek in a photon torpedo
    shot out toward the stars;
    the writer in a cardboard box
    filled with lost poems and unsold books;
    the earth-mother animal-lover
    in a tiny pet cemetery
    bound by brambles and tarnished chimes.
All these things I have been,
yet I am none of them.
They lie in crematory ashes,
withered images in old photographs,
words and phrases on a scratchy 8-track.
Stripped free of the ghosts,
all that remains is me:
    the whistle that lingers when the train is gone,
    the empty stage when the play is done,
    a blank page awaiting pen or brush.
A voice in my head whispers,
"You're finally dead."
Now it is time to live.

Whisperings From the Abyss

Spirits from other dimensions
sing pagan hymns
in the dark and musky choir loft
high atop the lost cathedral.
A chorus of wind through broken bottles,
soft whispering chants
best heard in madhouses at midnight.
Fingers of blanched bone
strum rusted piano wires
once used by lunatics
to strangle sleeping children
while drums strung with human leather,
still warm,
pound a little rhythm
like the footfalls of approaching death.
Deep in the night,
the new moon rises black,
the blind eye of a dead god
perceiving none of it.

Still Life

Frozen in amber fog,
an aftermath of storm,
the night is a still life
sculpted by street lights.
If I could walk between
these molecules of suspended mist,
into this motionless moment
of bare trees scratching phantom paradise
with broken fingers,
I think I could become
the thing I have always been.

Drug

So much like needles are your fangs,
delicate instruments of pain
tipped with morphine,
drawing out the soul's elixir,
injecting dreams.

Vagabond

A glint of metal beneath a streetlight,
shabby stranger on the road to neverland.
You're just a shadow man,
old metal tool box in your hand,
filled with all the gadgets and gizmos
that make the world keep spinning
and realign the rising moon
to compensate for falling stars
that throw chaos out of order
from time to time again and again.
The look in your eyes stops clocks,
the tux thrown over your shoulder
just another mystery,
the uniform you carry home from work.

The Last Supper

I scatter trick-or-treat candy
from street to altar,
muttering evocations and incantations
to raise you from the dead
and lead you home again.
A marshmallow pumpkin is your heart,
candy corn your fangs.
Cold cider flows thru pixie stick veins,
bittersweet blood
of the King of Halloween.
I ingest you reverently,
a humble acolyte
praying for transubstantiation.

Alchemy

It is a night of train whistles
blown a hundred years ago
echoing on the edge of a storm
sometime in this insignificant April.
I bathe in the cold,
rubbing shade and rain into my pores
until I resemble the silver nothing
found on the horizon at dusk.
Clouds dangle long wet fingers
to the ground,
and I dream of drinking blood
from nipples of fog and mist.
Vampyres tie celtic knots,
weaving a new ancient tapestry
of a delicate reality.
My grave lies empty
in some far future century,
and I sense myself dancing
on the madhouse balcony
where Time and Death
are only genies in a bottle,
imprisoned on the shaman's top shelf.

Footsteps

Desert silence so still
I sometimes hear moonbeams
walking on the windowsill,
padded yellow feet
writing the secret names
of misplaced demons
in settled dust and amber ash
from distant fires left burning
on the far shore of Time.

Wintersilk

Smoke is on the wind
and the spider is weaving winter silk again,
a death shroud tightly-knit.
Jack o'lanterns hold hands
in fields of goblin grass,
winking occasionally
to light the October path
and take photographs of Time.
The road to Amboy is haunted
with melancholy melodies
playing on a broken radio
rusting tenderly in the shattered dash
of a '55 Chevy.
Shadows with no earthly source
gather around me,
giving me shape and substance again.
On abandoned train tracks
I wait,
my soul in your pocket,
your blood in my veins.

Creation

I am black lipstick,
an injection of tongue
to warm your chilled mouth.
Pierce my lips with your teeth.
Reform me with fangs.
End my world.

Artifacts

Vampyre shaman worships stopped clocks
and builds night clubs over sundials
to trap time in a shadow.
Rain is a fallen seraphim
torn to a million tears.
We collect them in old stone jars,
putting the pieces together again,
holy water upon dark altar
where mortals come to spill their blood.

Umberlight

We live in a vampyre snow globe,
where shooting stars speak in tongues
and mushrooms conspire with Grandmother Spider
to hold the dayshine world away.
The capital city is Umberlight.
The king is known as Spades.
Here our factories manufacture night.
Our merchants peddle amnesia.

Death Sentence

The executioner here is known only
as The Unpronounceable Scream.
There are no sins in our city,
no crimes worthy of death
in a place where Death does not exist.
Nevertheless...
Business is brisk,
men and women alike
competing for the fatal kiss,
the blissful wickedness
of dying in these immortal arms,
impaled on carnal blade.

Prince of the City

The Prince of Fornever
was neither elected nor born,
but ascended the throne
by creating Himself with a kiss
of cold lips to his own torn wrist
long before the jealous gods
took their first trembling breath.

It is said he holds court
in the Parish of Nethershadows,
sorting acorns and quantum things,
deciding the fate of faeries,
the outcome of Eternity.

Once upon a fragment in Time,
I thought I heard him singing,
but it was only a whirlwind
crossing the bridge
between the prison at Dayshine
and the unharvested garden
of All That Is Possible.

Keeping Time

Our seasons are measured
by the tails and tales of comets,
the breadth and breath
of Lost Tomorrows.

Deep in the Fog Forest,
the Earl of Everautumn
dreams the birth of eternity:
   future history whispered
    on the tongues of ravens,
hatched from the egg of a sylph.

Reality is only a tumbleweed,
fragmented and fatally fractured.
All that is real
is the harlequin's will,
spinning the warlock's Dream.

The Law of Autumn in Umberlight

Halloween comes every Sun-day
though the sun is not permitted to rise.
We worship at the altar of irony,
drink our sacrament from goblets of paradox.
The scarecrow dines on orange embers,
while Smoketree Farm is flayed alive
by haunted windmill shadows.

Asylum in Umberlight

The winter holiday is known as Asylum,
not for any reason
but because that's how it's always been.
Carols are sung by hallucinations posing as children
and the Mayor of Mourning rings thirteen bells
at the mid of night on Asylum's Eve.

If a raven comes to your window calling
with sprig of poison holly,
you'll know that you've been chosen
to live forever in Umbernight
now and forever existing
at the fingertips of your magick.

Tarot

You are the Priest of Fevers and long-dead roses,
pacing the midnight in your parish of shadows
while the Nun of Nothingness hums pagan hymns
and counts lost souls on her blood-drop rosary.
The scythe lies idle
and funeral mass is not spoken here,
Death having been dealt his own card at last.

Postcard

The whole world is a postcard
sent by a maniac
outside of time's asylum.
The fiend wears my face
and has mushrooms for eyes.
Reality evaporates,
a drop of blood
drying in the sun.

Addict

The stars are only drawings
inside the lid of my coffin,
needlemarks on the arm
of a junkie god
addicted to death.

Going, Going, Gone

There's an immortal trance dancing
on the ceiling above my dreaming
and the clocks are running backwards
trying to keep up with paradoxes and entropy.
I think I've gone crazy
because all of this seems far more reasonable
than dayshine scripts
and fairy tale religions
where virgins give birth to God.
White picket fences are only cages
and all the world's a coffin
floating down a river of stars.

The Tao

I am the tao of shadows,
black paint on ebony canvas,
moon chariot drawing the terminator
over illusions of heaven and earth.
A blanket of stars
blinds the sun.

~

A scattering of streetlights
blooms along an empty road,
wildflowers of the night
harvested by vampyres with slingshots.
It's raining petals of shattered glass.

Twigs

It is the annual harvest
of cobwebs and meteors,
a time of gathering dry twigs
and tall tales.
Darklings are rearranging the constellations
while mortals open the seasons
like greeting cards
that all too quickly
crumble to dust.

Why Immortals Weep

Ships of the dead
laden with fugitive souls
sail this black blood river
lined with bones of the damned.
You captain the fleet
from the bow of Marie Celeste,
your shirt a tattered silk sail,
the feather in your hat
plucked from Lucifer's wing.
You tell me
the journey has no destination
except the reflection
always changing in my eye,
for the world of illusions lies in ruins,
all her children only tears on the faces of angels.
Now I know why you weep:
   to keep the world alive,
   an island in the abyss,
   even if only a mirage.

Lady In Waiting

I summon you from the underworld,
you with pentacles for eyes
and fallen stars smoldering on your fingertips
and immortal blood
harvested from the River Styx.
In the desert tonight,
the winds are calm as a cyclone,
still as the screams
echoing off the cold black flesh
of the abyss.
I have counted all the grains of sand
in the hourglass of my life
and sorted all the scattered petals
gathered from mildewed sepulchres.
And still you wait,
a silence in the shadows,
a space in the emptiness.

Double, Double

On the dusky outskirts
of the City of October,
beyond the last bend
of a dead-end road
named Eternity's Beginning,
on the edge of a cliff
where shadows and substance
conspire to snatch the stopwatch
carried in the tattered pocket of Time,
you sit dangling fish hooks
baited with scraps of poetry
into the shattered crystal mirror
of the madhouse mortal continuum,
trolling for lost souls
whose only salvation is undead damnation.

The Cleansing

I need a bath of shadows
to get the sun off my skin.
The water is made
of black shade
kept in the closet
and under the bed.
Tonight
I will be clean again.

The Unborn

My blood is full of poems
red wet children
waiting to be born
on your tongue.
Love me to death and back
to set the words free.
It's vampyre season,
the black eggs ripe in time for Easter.

The harvest begins at moon-up,
hatchlings nipped from umbilical vine
by the nurturing teeth
of the darkling king.
The fruit is shipped in coffin crates
labeled for Eternity
and packed on board the ghost train
that steals through small towns
and fitful fever dreams,
carrying its cargo of pale fiends
back and forth through always-autumn.

Late last night you can hear them singing-
hymns with no words or rhyme.
The brute with the scythe
is crucified to the tracks,
his screams only a lonely whistle
at a weedy cemetery's edge where
a single headstone bears his epitaph:
        "Hail immortality, death is dead!"

Carnival Dark

A carnival blew into raggedy land
on a breath of winter wind.
The Tilt-a-Whirl paints movies in light
across the canopy of night
and stars are self-igniting candles
burning only to watch themselves burn out.
Smoke from carny lips
draws misbegotten mist,
so there are always whispers from nowhere:
"Hey, you!"
"Over here!"
"Want a ride, little girl?"
But you turn around and no one's there.
The darkling king sells cotton candy
to the dentist's daughter
and rides the ferris wheel alone till dawn.
The night sky cries, making rain
to oil the gears
of the noisy generators of time.

Tomorrow's Dust

Winsome wind moves
through molecules of mist,
at home nowhere.
It says it's stirring the dust
to make sure it settles properly
in old coffee cups
and atop unread books.
I write the secret name
of the darkling king
on a cracked wood windowsill--
a haunted room where blood drips,
heard but never seen.
Time is running away,
looking for a thin place to hide.
Reality is a movie of the week,
cheaply made.

False Autumn

False autumn lingers,
a transfusion to strengthen my blood.
Let me feed you
the red petals of me,
the veins in the falling leaves
of my wayward thoughts and dreams.

Warnings to the Living

Rain has washed the stars away again,
leaving only a grey mist canvas
where ghosts write their names
with melted silver crayons,
madhouse messages on slaughterhouse walls,
warnings to the living
that Death loves unfinished poems.

Oh, Lonely Night

The darkling king sits alone tonight,
his only company an audience of sepulchres.
He polishes his crown
with a funeral shroud,
weeping to the empty road
worn thin as silk
by immortal footsteps.

Unholy Communion

"Eat my body," you whisper,
tearing a pallid wrist.
"Drink of Death and be immune to it."
I wear your stain on my lips
and will share your grave at dawn.

If

I bathe in shadows,
rubbing the night into my skin.
Powder from a moth's wings
dusts my cheeks
and whispers of the damned carry on the mist.
They say you're out there on the road,
admiring your reflection in broken mirrors,
peeking in my dirty windows,
looking to see if you see yourself
living a life that might have been
if you were a man instead of the darkling king.

Back to the Boat

A voice passing through the nothing whispers,
"We have to get back to the boat."
A twin-rigger she was,
with timbers creaking beneath our feet
on a sea so still
we gazed down into the midnight sky,
dizzying refracted realities,
and the ship had become a starswimmer,
and all the stars just trinkets on your belt.
Your eyes were stolen sapphires,
your heart a pagan drum
stretched taut over the hollow
of vacant crypts and empty coffins
where our bones would be writing
sonnets of dust
had we never embarked on this treacherous trip.
"We have to get back to the boat."
Back to that place
where the rivers of reason have all run dry,
where silence has its own continuum,
and the flesh we inhabit is luminous silver,
where all of creation is our address,
all of time our identity.

The Effect of Moonlight on Tombstones

The world has rolled on her side
and put on October clothes:
   faded umber gown, brittle as glass,
   tattered lace made of sea foam,
   veils of fog curling past chimneys
   where the season's first fire
   spells out messages
   in smoke and spark.
The door between realities
stands open a crack,
revealing the shadows still to come,
the effect of moonlight on tombstones.

About the Author...

Della Van Hise is a native of Florida, transplanted to California at the age of 21, who has subsequently sunk her roots into the desert near Joshua Tree National Park. She has not personally seen any aliens since around 1992, but there is rumored to be a secret UFO base underneath her house.

Della's writing started around age 11 on an old Smith Corona typewriter. No, not an electric one. A real antique, made of metal and heavier than a wet coffin. Her first professional novel was best-selling KILLING TIME - the controversial Star Trek novel which was recalled and re-edited in 1984 (making the first edition a rare collector's item) - and which was the foundational plot for the first STAR TREK "Reboot" movie.

Della has written extensively in the non-fiction genre, with titles such as *Quantum Shaman* and *Scrawls On the Walls of the Soul*. *Quantum Shaman* focuses heavily on the author's metaphysical explorations and experiences, while *Scrawls* is a continuation of those journeys many years later. If you enjoyed the works of Carlos Castaneda or Don Miguel Ruiz, you'll enjoy the non-fiction works of Della Van Hise.

In addition, Della has written professionally for Tomorrow Magazine and other prominent science fiction publications. Her most recent fiction works include *Sons of Neverland* (an award-winning vampire novel); *No Forwarding Address* (a science fiction quest of the heart's yearning); and Coyote (a young adult novel combining the mystical aspects of martial arts, coming of age, and personal sacrifice.)

Della shares her life with her significant other, Wendy Rathbone, and a variety of cats, dogs and desert wildlife.

Other titles from Eye Scry Publications...

SONS OF NEVERLAND
an erotic vampyre novel
by Della Van Hise

"The virtuosity shown here is only the beginning of a pyrotechnic talent unfolding into the hidden dimensions of the human and nonhuman spirit."
                -Jacqueline Lichtenberg

"What Sons of Neverland resembled to me was the creative hagiographies of Nikos Kazantzakis, where a few stylized characters deliver a message that goes way beyond the parameter of the characters themselves. And much like Kazantzakis, this book zones on the question of immortality. However, this is not just the decadent historical immortality of the long-lived vampire, it is immortality as a change in one's perception. This is the story behind the story, delivered by characters that are hyper-real - each one loaded with symbolism. Sons of Neverland will have you filled, even brimming over with the sense of Mysterium Tremendum et Fascinans. Go there for a full helping of the numinous." (A Reviewer on Amazon!)

Set against a backdrop of contemporary culture, SONS OF NEVERLAND explores the universal questions of life & death, sex & love - the most crucial challenges every human being faces - through the eyes of the immortal vampire.

The novella "Kiss of the Black Angel" is available for free on Kindle – a preview to SONS OF NEVERLAND.

www.eyescrypublications.com

www.amazon.com/Sons-Neverland-Della-Van-Hise-ebook/dp/B00O4GUH2W/

"If Prince of Umberlight doesn't rattle your cage, you're more dead than the undead!" -**Night Readers**

Thorn may be an 800 year old vampire, but he does not possess the ability to create others of his kind, and so he is cursed to fall in love with mortals, only to watch them grow old and die. Torn by grief, Thorn denounces his immortality and enters into a comatose oblivion for decades. When he awakens, he is no longer in London, but finds himself in a world spun into being by his own desires - a world where Time and Death do not exist, a world where it is forever autumn, where the Parish of Shadows and the River of Stars become his home. It is in this world of Umberlight that he meets Atom - an interloper into his private sanctuary, but also an impudent imp who is destined to reveal to Thorn the three dangerous elements a vampire must possess in order to become a Creator.

The Art of Brutality.
Submission to Dark Desire.
Love.

FROM THE AUTHOR
www.eyescrypublications.com

ON AMAZON
http://www.amazon.com/Prince-Umberlight-Tales-Book-ebook/dp/B00TRD2EHS/ref=asap_bc?ie=UTF8

NO FORWARDING ADDRESS
Della Van Hise

When Terrans came to sail dark seas,
And see what stars might be...
Heaven moved with no forwarding
address,
And left this void to me.
(Children's song from Lazali)

A literary science fiction novel told in the voice of an empath, *No Forwarding Address* explores the lures and the dangers of love, the tragedies and triumphs stirring in the human heart.

When Crystal and Raine first meet, it is 50 years after The Great War on Earth. They are hesitant to trust, afraid to love. But even if they are able to overcome these seemingly insurmountable obstacles, is even love enough?

When a man has the stars in his eyes, legend says he must serve them above all others.

I knew then that it wasn't love and hate who were mirror twins. The final irony was that grief would always turn out to be the paradoxical antithesis and simultaneous manifestation of whatever it is that humans call love.

Crystal remained silent and walked a few steps away from Raine – further down the shoreline, until she stood under the wing of one fallen Phantom. She thought of the ship she had seen from the balcony of our home, and though it had long since disappeared over the dark and treacherous abyss of the ocean, its image lingered clearly in her thoughts. On that ship was a man, she thought. A terribly lonely man who made no great difference to the flow of time or the memory of the galaxy. A man who, like Raine, was compelled to keep moving and look only ahead and never behind. A man who could not afford the luxury of waving goodbye to friends on shore.

At last, she turned toward her beloved and watched him watching the darkness. He stood only a few feet away, yet the images in my mind said he might as well have been a million light years off in the void. He was lost to her in that instant out-of-time, just as lost and impossible to find as the light from that ship which had vanished over the horizon...

www.eyescrypublications.com
http://www.amazon.com/Forwarding-Address-Della-Van-Hise-ebook/dp/B00PEOSKJ0/

COYOTE
Della Van Hise

A Novel of Love, Honor and Personal Sacrifice...

When River Willows is accused of a murder she didn't commit, her life takes a turn toward the sanctuary of a world existing at right-angles to our own. Combining the mysticism of martial arts and the romantic conflict of a young woman torn between two powerful men, COYOTE takes the reader on an epic journey of dangerous secrets, military cover-ups, and the infinite heart of the peaceful warrior.

"So who's Coyote?" I asked, trying to ignore the effect he was having on me. "You?"

Steale laughed easily, though it did little to hide the torment behind that mask of indifference he wore so well.

"Coyote's a scavenger, Jack of all trades. The Native Americans call him the trickster - the one who brought chaos down on the world." He shrugged as if altogether unconcerned. "Original sin."

"Is that what you are?" I asked, keeping it light despite the growing knot my stomach. "Original sin?"

He kept his profile to me, eyes straight ahead as he drove. "Sure you want to know?"

I couldn't help wondering if I had cornered the coyote, or if the clever trickster had cornered me.

By the author of **KILLING TIME** – without a doubt the most controversial **STAR TREK** novel ever published!

From the author:
www.eyescrypublications.com

On Amazon
http://www.amazon.com/Coyote-Della-Van-Hise/dp/0976689782/

YEAR OF THE RAM
Della Van Hise

Year of the Ram was described by one reviewer as... "A spacefaring gay romance full of love, angst, and longing."

Only after Star Commander Morgan Diego becomes an exile as a result of a Galaxy Corps political blunder does he begin to realize how much he valued the companionship of his second in command - the mysterious Lucien, an Alfarian who is more elven than human, with peculiar powers & abilities which begin to unfold as he, too, realizes what he has lost.

Separated by circumstance from his former life, Morgan is thrust into a world where he must survive by his wits. When he meets a peculiar little old man calling himself Kim Le, Morgan finds himself in a situation where he is required to master The Art - not only a form of human & extraterrestrial martial arts, but a way of living and being that will alter his life forever.

At the temple, he is introduced to his new teacher, another Alfarian who begins to steal his heart - a heart which is already promised to Lucien. Torn and conflicted, Morgan struggles with the world he left behind and the world he now inhabits.

Beginning to believe he may never again return to his ship and to the friends and loved ones he left behind, he is all the more frustrated and heartbroken when a new Master arrives at the temple: a man to whom Morgan is immediately drawn both mentally and physically, a man who is strikingly familiar... yet utterly alien.

Year of the Ram is a fully-fleshed novel, approximately 97000 words, with a focus on the love story and romance angle. Set against a science fiction milieu, it explores the infinite possibilities of the human and alien heart. Sexual content is explicit, though is not the primary focus of the novel.

For those who like a romance that forces its characters to contemplate the ecstasies AND the agonies of love... you will enjoy *Year of the Ram* immensely.

FROM THE AUTHOR:
www.eyescrypublications.com

ON AMAZON:
http://www.amazon.com/Year-Ram-Della-Van-Hise/dp/0989693813/

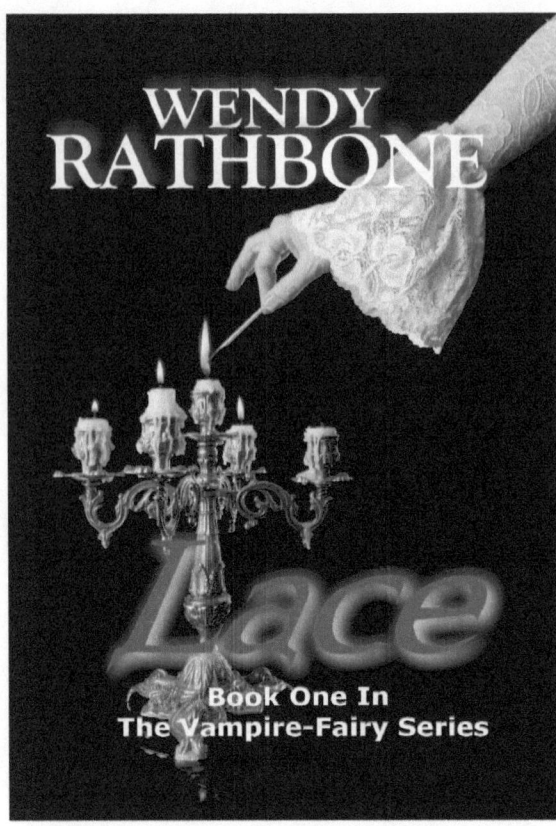

LACE
Wendy Rathbone

Lace is a being from another dimension on Earth. He cannot die and humans call his kind "vampire" and declare war on them.

Firi is a human military soldier, a trained guard, who has met Lace twice in his young life and formed a bond with him.

In a world where humans and vampires are arch enemies, where vampires are eradicated in horrible ways, where being a vampire-lover means a death sentence, can Firi and Lace ever find each other again and explore the feelings they have for each other?

Will Lace be able escape his government prison, and the amnesia that keeps him from accessing his true powers?

Can Firi, the boy he met in the woods ten years ago, ever hope to help him?

A male/male romance about secrets that can get you killed, impossible rescues, and old lovers who cannot be trusted.

On Amazon
https://www.facebook.com/groups/Carlos.Castaneda.group/

From the Author
www.eyescrypublications.com

SCOUNDREL
Wendy Rathbone

Antares is a willing sex slave, trained in the harems of Anada since the age of 18, and owned by a wealthy master who spoils his slaves. But all that changes when Empire soldiers invade Antares' world and he is taken away from the only life he's ever known.

In a colonized galaxy where starships are as common as houseflies, and a dark Empire seeks to control thousands of civilized worlds, there are those who fall through the cracks and refuse to be conquered, including the pirate, Slate, and his crew.

Out in the darkness of the unknown, among Empire soldiers and scoundrels, will bad fates befall Antares and his fellow captive companions?

Will Slate finally find the love he's been looking for his whole life?

Can Slate and Antares ever see eye to eye?

On Amazon
http://www.amazon.com/Scoundrel-Wendy-Rathbone-ebook/dp/B014BU7V42/ref=asap_bc?ie=UTF8

From the Author
http://www.eyescrypublications.com

LETTERS TO AN ANDROID
Wendy Rathbone

Cobalt is a created human, vat grown and born adult, with no human rights and indentured to serve others for the duration of his life. Liyan is a young man with wanderlust in his eyes, embarking on a career that takes him to the furthest regions of space. The two become unlikely friends and create a memorable long-distance correspondence. Through Liyan, Cobalt gets to explore the universe, living vicariously through his friend's wave transmissions. A strong bond develops between them that not even the stars can put asunder.

Now you know an android who writes poetry.

This is all your fault. Did you not read my last wave telling you extracurricular activities for my kind are discouraged? Of course this is harmless and strangely enjoyable and does not necessarily require me to leave the hotel. Pel would not care if I wrote lines of equations or nonsensical juxtaposed words. As long as the act does not bring my mental state into question.

However, in history, poetry is often written by the rebels.

So we can keep this to ourselves.

Let me know about your lieutenant's test.

And to give you peace of mind, I never believed you observed me as anything other than human.

Some people are and always will be hateful bigots. Most people are simply uncomfortable in speaking to "property." And anyway, friendship, like poetry, is also discouraged.

Your friend,
Cobalt

FROM THE AUTHOR:
www.eyescrypublications.com

ON AMAZON:
http://www.amazon.com/Letters-Android-Wendy-Rathbone/dp/0989693872/

PALE ZENITH
Wendy Rathbone
A Science Fiction Novel

On a far-flung "Earth" in a parallel universe, two factions are fighting a decades-long psychic war. Young talented psychics are being temporarily kidnapped from present day Earth, seemingly at random, to serve as part of one side's psychic army. They are put under the control of spychiatrists, mysterious machines with many limbs that have a programmed ability to travel time and space and universes to kidnap and control carefully selected humans. The humans never know they are being used; when their missions are completed they are brought back to their universe through time and placed back in their beds, their memories wiped.

———————————

The shadows wound the tall corridor in muted gold, varnished brown. It seemed as though they were in the bowels of a giant serpent coiled outside time, outside space.

When they left the palace, a familiar sun flourished in a clear, blue sky. But this wasn't their sun. Not Zack's sun. It was an alien star burning within a different galaxy in an all too distant universe. Zack looked up squinting, trying to see if he could peer beyond the sky, beyond the pale of midday and into his own timespace, but there was nothing. Only sunlight. Only the thin atmosphere of an Earth not his own.

His back knotted again. Leo's presence was a gelid space inside his chest, empty. Always before he'd felt a warmth there, a sort of pressure like someone's hand pressed gently to his heart. He'd taken Leo for granted knowing, the way a shadow falls when you block the sun, that he was there around him, inside him: blood, air, salt, brain, soul. They were genetic duplicates, twins, spiritual halves. Without him, Zack knew the first icy tugs of panic.

FROM THE AUTHOR
www.eyescrypublications.com
ON AMAZON
http://www.amazon.com/Pale-Zenith-Wendy-Rathbone/dp/0976689790/

The Foundling
by Wendy Rathbone

Diego is a powerful man with a tragic past. Out on the expansive ocean in his private yacht, he discovers a beautiful and mysterious man adrift on a raft, near death. The bond that forms between them in the aftermath of Alec's rescue is one of fierce passion, though lacking in trust. Can they make it work, or will Alec's amnesia bring forth secrets so disturbing as to tear them apart? A passionately erotic love story of desire and darkness, exquisite and explicit.

I can see his struggle between gratitude and uneasiness. He is buffeted by all things new and strange. He does not know where he is from, who he is or what happened to him. He does not know me. There has not been enough time to transition between strangers and friendship.

This isolation of his is something I can identify with, but it is also a feeling no one can help him with until or unless he gets his own life back. And his memory.

If that doesn't happen, then it will take time for him to build a new life. He is polite to me, even friendly, but even a night together during a storm with his arms wrapped tight around my waist doesn't calm the surge I see inside him, the emptiness, the loss, possibly even panic. That night may have reinforced some trust in me, but so far not enough for him to completely relax.

He seeks me out, though. That's something. He sits by me at dinner when he can have any seat of his choosing. I watch him closely when he does not realize it. At dinner the following night after we had only 'slept' together, and before we go to bed again in separate rooms, I notice everything about him, how he moves, the way the air warms when he is closer to me, the dry sheen of his lips as they part for more air when he is reacting to something, or speaking, or eating.

His hands still shake. Anyone else might not notice because he keeps them clasped into fists at his sides or, while sitting, pressed tight to his lap.

I spend another fretful night alone. I dream restlessly, wild, loud and colorful visions I cannot recall at all as soon as my eyes open. All I know is the dreams leave me unfulfilled, impatient.

www.eyescry.com/html/publications.htm

None Can Hold the Dark
Wendy Rathbone

In the eagerly-awaited sequel to Wendy Rathbone's homoerotic romance ***"The Foundling,"*** Diego and Alec meet new challenges in private and from the outside world. Diego is being investigated by the local police for murder. Meanwhile, Alec's amnesia and the trauma of his kidnapping by white slavers continue to plague him. And the danger to Alec is not yet over.

Distracted by their new love, both men fail to see certain threats until it is almost too late.

"Why do you keep doing this illegal business?" Now Alec's gaze turned toward him, open as the day and lit with a sad frenzy, a challenge. "You could go anywhere, do anything, be anyone."

Diego had asked himself that question on rare occasions. In truth, he got used to what he was, what he did. Even a dangerous known was perhaps preferable to the unknown. "People depend on me."

Alec shook his head, but smiled a little as he said, "That's so weak." He leaned forward, over the arm of the chair, and put his shaking hand on the back of Diego's head. The kiss was cool, lingering, moist with salt. When Alec pulled back, he said almost matter of factly, "It's like there's sharks and there's goldfish and one can't decide to become the other."

Diego was still stunned by the kiss. But the words hit him hard. In them was the unfair conjecture of a locked fate. He believed in making his own fate...or luck. Did Alec think only one kind of man lived inside him and that was all there was to it? To life? It hurt. Badly.

Diego sat back on his heels, catching himself with his hands on the smooth floor. "So, Alec, which am I?"

Alec frowned.

Diego said, "I made choices in my life. I made them No one made them for me. If I need to be strong I'm strong. If I need to be vicious I can be that too. So what? I'm stuck there? In a pattern, a role...with no free will?"

Alec watched him inquisitively now.

"Because," Diego went on, "I'm solely responsible for my actions. Me. Could you say the same of the shark?"

They both waited, the silence covering them in muggy discomfort.

"You think you understand me?" Diego finally asked.

www.eyescrypublications.com

The Lostling: Alec's Story
Book Three in The Foundling Trilogy
by *Wendy Rathbone*

The Lostling takes place directly after *None Can Hold the Dark*, as Alec and Diego relocate to San Francisco. There, amid salty winter wind and fog, Alec's lost memories slowly return and he must relive some of his most painful and terrifying moments to regain his forgotten self. In agonizing dreams and flashes of memory, he finally remembers what happened to him... and why.

Excerpt: *Putting a hand on his arm or leg, I can always feel the tremor of Diego even through his clothes, an innate wildness, a life-power.*

I always believed, from the first day Diego found me unconscious and dying, floating in the middle of a sapphire Caribbean ocean, there was a core of me unhidden, unforgotten, that cried out silently to the air and everything around me communicating who I am, what I am.

I can't remember it myself. Not that core, not anything up to the day I awoke in Diego's bed, sick and panicked. In that moment, I remembered nothing more than my first name, and even that memory is suspect. But this core of me demands to take things into its own hands to be seen, to make sure it remains "I am."

I believe Diego saw it, the urgent desperation in me wanting to be witnessed, and he made a promise to that essence of me, to that heart of me, that he would see me through anything that came my way. Something in me reached up and latched onto him, a clasping energy, and Diego clasped back.

It caught and held him. He was moved. He was compelled. He was mesmerized.

www.eyescrypublications.com

http://www.amazon.com/Lostling-Alecs-Story-Foundling-Book-ebook/dp/B00RO8GSUW/

UNEARTHLY
by Wendy Rathbone

A Collection of Award-Winning Poetry

Intro by the Author: This book contains all my out of print chapbooks (mini-collections of an author's work usually published by smaller presses.)

The chapbooks published within include:
Moon Canoes, published by Dark Regions Press, 1994
(Im)mortal, published by Shadowfire Press, 1996
Scrying The River Styx, published by Anamnesis Press, 1999
Autumn Phantoms, published by Flesh and Blood Press, 2000
Dreams of Decadence Presents: Wendy Rathbone, published by DNA Publications 2002
Dancing in the Haunted Woodlands, published by Yellow Bat Review, 2003
Vampyria, published by Eye Scry Publications, 2005

She Sleeps With Vampires
She sleeps with vampires
courting velvet breaths
poem-dreams
chill-stopped hearts

Wrapped in her arms
like teddy bear thoughts
purple lips trembling
at her quiet throat
they love her more than
somber rain
more than autumn
more than ash-soft hearths of night.

FROM THE AUTHOR
www.eyescrypublications.com

ON AMAZON
http://www.amazon.com/Unearthly-Wendy-Rathbone-ebook/dp/B00B0MTIZK/

Non-fiction titles from Eye Scry Publications...

TEACHINGS OF THE IMMORTALS
by Mikal Nyght

So... You Want To Live Forever?
The teachings are presented as brief vignettes in no particular order of importance. This is not a book you read from start to finish in a single night. It is a grimoire of self-creation, intended to be contemplated slowly so as to be assimilated wholly. Pick it up and turn to a page at random. Where your eyes come to rest on the page is your lesson for the day. Go no further until you have assimilated the lesson totally.

The teachings are seduction as much as instruction. This is the way of The Dark Evolution.

The Ruby Slippers

The danger of the consensual continuum is that its natural gravity exists at the lowest common denominator of human experience, and because of this it will automatically make you forget those elusive truths you've fought to learn, and before you know it you're lost in petty dramas again, sinking into the mire of old familiar scripts.

The only way to overcome this is to be continually cavorting with worlds and events beyond human experience, journeying into the unknown so that it can become known, expanding knowledge and awareness to become more than you were, bringing back from the Dreaming those secrets which will teach you how to use the ruby slippers to transport yourself over the rainbow to the vampyre wizard's secret lair.

Perception

This is the nature of reality: to be precisely what perception dictates, as solid and whole as your interpretation of it, or as changeable and eternal as you permit it to be.

It wasn't knowledge god tried to keep from Man, you see. It was perception, for perception alone has the power to destroy god and obliterate comfortable consensual realities to create unending immortality.

Take the apple, my embryonic children. Nibble its red red flesh.

Open your vampyre eyes so you may finally begin to *See*.

www.immortalis-animus.com
www.eyescrypublications.com

http://www.amazon.com/Teachings-Immortals-Mikal-Nyght-ebook/dp/B00C2HY5WS/

Quantum Shaman:
Diary of a Nagual Woman
Della Van Hise\

"Diary of a Nagual Woman brings a quantum understanding to what has traditionally been believed to be a mystical path alone. This book picks up where Carlos Castaneda left off to take us on a roller coaster ride of our own forgotten power..." - Michael Grove, Reviewer

When I asked how Orlando had known I would come to this remote location, and how he himself had gotten there – since there were no other cars in the tiny parking lot – he only smiled a little, stretched out his long legs, and slouched down on that cold metal bench to stare up at the stars.

"You're predictable," he said as if I should have already known. "I'm here because this is where you always come when you're mad at the world."

I attempted to engage him in a conversation of just exactly how he knew I was mad at the world, since I'd had no direct contact with him in quite some time, nothing to give him any hint of what was going on in my everyday life. But even as I began spelling all of that out to him, he brushed my words aside with an easy gesture.

"Do you want to talk or do you want to waste time looking for logical explanations for every magical thing that ever happens?" he asked. "That's what's wrong with the world, you know. Instead of embracing the mysteries and trying to determine how they might open a crack in an otherwise humdrum, pre-programmed existence, people waste their entire lives explaining it all away, attaching labels to it, filing and categorizing it until it loses any meaning."

He had a point. And I'd already been inundated with enough mysteries to know that some things simply had no explanation humans could understand. *'Magic is only science not yet understood'.* Words Orlando had written more than a year before rattled through my mind up there in the middle of the night, in the middle of nowhere, looking down on a distant world that seemed far more unreal to me at that moment than the world he had been trying to teach me to *see*.

He was there – whether physically or in some spirit-form is ultimately\ of no importance, for in the sorcerer's world there is no difference between body and spirit, and in any world, perception is reality.

www.quantumshaman.com
www.eyescrypublications.com

Scrawls on the Walls of the Soul
Della Van Hise

The long-awaited follow-up to
Quantum Shaman: Diary of a Nagual Woman.
Stands alone, or order together!

"If you've ever felt like a stranger in a strange land, this book is your road map to survival in the spiritual wilderness!" (Michael Grove)

~

It was May of 2000 when my mentor threw me out of the quantum cosmic classroom and said, "I've taught you everything I can. Now it's time to take that knowledge and slam it up against the walls of the real world. If it remains intact and survives the brutality to which it will be subjected, you will get a gold star next to your name and be allowed to proceed to the next level." No mention was made of what this next level might be, or if, indeed, it truly existed.

Go ahead – try to explain this all-consuming path to your friends and relatives. They will smile politely, squirm uncomfortably, and eventually they will stop returning your phone calls and look the other way when they see you coming. And who can blame them? They live in the real world with their office jobs and nuclear families and a host of mindless sitcoms waiting on the propaganda box at the end of their busy day. In direct contrast, it could be observed that anyone who has dedicated themselves to the pursuit of forbidden knowledge really doesn't live in that world at all. Not for lack of wanting, perhaps, but because the real world is quickly seen to be little more than a series of programs and illusions – not unlike The Matrix. And not surprisingly, the people who populate that world may begin to take on a peculiar zombie-like quality.

You find yourself alone in a world of jesters, jokers and jackasses. Now what?

FROM THE AUTHOR
www.quantumshaman.com

ON AMAZON
http://www.amazon.com/Scrawls-Walls-Soul-Della-Hise-ebook/dp/B008CUKH6C/

Eye Scry Publications
A Visionary Publishing Company
www.eyescrypublications.com

www.ingramcontent.com/pod-product-compliance
Lightning Source LLC
Chambersburg PA
CBHW020544130626
46552CB00007B/2749